Letters :

My Name Is Egypt

And This Is My Very First Book

by Egypt

Letters From The Dog

My Name Is Egypt
And This Is My Very First Book

Copyright © 2011 Marian Glaser

ISBN 978-1-60458-805-7

Printed in the United States by InstantPublisher.com

Dedication

To my Doctor

Deborah A. O'Keefe, DVM, MS, DACVIM
Diplomat

Board Certified in Internal Medicine and Oncology

Whose special medical skills and kindness kept me alive and made me healthy again, I am grateful

Egypt

Acknowledgements:

This little book has been two years in the making. There have been countless writings and rewritings.

There have been readings and more readings, and edits and more edits. So many friends have helped with this, the final edit, that I cannot name them all. But they all know who they are and will be forever written in Egypt's heart and in mine, too.

Egypt and I will be forever grateful for such great friends.

We do want to acknowledge in a special way, our friend, Connie Maedel-Diehl of Maedel Photo here in Monroe, Michigan. All the beautiful studio portraits of Egypt are her work. Egypt loved to pose for her.

The cover photograph is by Pamela Smith, Finer Arts Photography. Other photos were given to us by friends and family and we have permission to use all.

A friend picked me out and gave me to Marian. I was rejected and given away. I was re-rejected and returned. So, what was I to do? I decided to be good

I sat on Marian's foot, I sat on her lap, and I wagged my tail a lot. I became her only shadow, and who can give away their only shadow?

I am here forever now and life is good. I invite you to read my book and taste life as I do!

Let me tell you a little about myself and then I will tell you how this book came to be.

This is ME:

I am five years old and my name is EGYPT.

I am an English Cocker Spaniel and this is my very first book. I will tell you a little more about me in just a moment but first let me tell you about my People Person, Marian.

My People Person (and doesn't everybody have one) is very nice and I love her very much. You would love her too if you knew her like I do. My People Person is a retired social worker. Now, she says she is retired but that is only partly true. You see, she still works weekends, and you should see what that does to MY schedule, but that is another story, for another time.

It is a good thing that she only works part time otherwise she couldn't live at the English Cocker Spaniel Retirement Home.

Well, actually it's her home, so I can't make the rules and, I suppose that at five years old I really can't consider retirement.

My People Person says that she feels older than God but nobody knows how old God is, do they? I worry about her working and I don't know how old she really is, but how old is too old to work anyway?

She still has a driver's license and that is a good sign, I think. As much as I would like to know how old she is, I can't read her drivers license because I am only five and don't know how to read yet.

Oh well, who cares anyway. This is my People Person and she helped me write this book. So I hope you enjoy it.

Sincerely,
Egypt

4

Table of Contents:

This was written by my People Person. I don't know why this is called a table of contents. It is a list. Last time I checked, tables have food on them! Sometimes my people person and I disagree on important stuff.

My List of LETTERS

Part I (My Story)

Part II (Me, A therapy Dog?)

Part I

Introduction (How I came to be me)

I was born in Detroit and I lived in Southfield for four
of my five years. I had a good life with my first people
person, Bill. We ate and played together anytime we
wanted to. We went on walks. We watched baseball
together. We napped. We visited around. We played
'Catch and Fetch' a lot. It really was a great life.

Then, one day, Bill told me he had to move to a
veteran's home, and, since I wasn't a veteran, I
couldn't go. So he had to find me a new home. He
contacted the English Cocker Spaniel Rescue People
Person and, even though I was a mix (more about
that later) the People Person found Marcia and
Marian in Monroe, Michigan.

Since I lived in Southfield, they drove up to see me
and, let me tell you, it almost wasn't a match! Marian
took one look at me and said, "She has a tail and her
legs are too long. She is too fat and, besides that, she

is wild." Marcia said, "She has cute feet..." Bill said, "Well, ladies, can I put her in your car?" Marcia said, "Yes!" while Marian was still shaking her head, but, reluctantly she let me in.

So here I was, going off in this strange car, (but it _was_ a Lincoln) and it looked like it might be an adventure. After all what did I have to lose? So off I went to Monroe.

Well, I almost lost a lot. In fact, I almost lost it all. We three got to the apartment complex and Marian took me for a walk, after exclaiming to Marcia that this would never work out. On this walk, Marian and I met a family and they had a cute little teacup dog.

The family fell in love with me. Marian happened to say, offhandedly: "Well, would you like to have her and take her home with you?" The whole family, that is, all except the teacup dog, said, "Oh yes, please let us have Egypt!"

So away I went again and didn't even get to spend the first night with Marian and Marcia.

Zoie, the Tea Cup dog, barked and nipped at me and I don't know why.......

This was turning out to be a bigger adventure than I thought! So the story continues....

At nine o'clock the next morning I am back with Marcia and Marian. The teacup dog hated me and her mother was afraid to leave me alone with her so she brought me back and I am still with Marian today. Thank goodness!

That nice family came back to see Marian a few days later and they had a visit. I came outside with Marian and listened quietly, sitting right by her side while she held my leash. They asked if they could take me for a walk and Marian said: "Oh that would be nice" as she handed over my leash and went inside.

Well, let me tell you, nobody asked ME if I wanted to go for a walk with THEM, so I just sat right down and refused to budge. After getting the message, they had to ring the doorbell and return me to Marian. They haven't been back since.

At some point you have to make a stand as to who your people person is going to be. So that was that, Marian and I are together now. It would turn out to be a new life and a new beginning for both us.

It took a few nights practice and begging but soon I was sleeping with Marian in the king-sized bed, even though Bill told her I always slept on the floor. Ha! I took care of that. The bed is better than any old floor, especially if it's your people person's bed, and don't let any doggie tell you differently.

We stayed at this place about a year. Then we got a new house with a big backyard, a golf course and my very own doggie door. Life was good at first, but then Marcia went away and it got very quiet for a very long time.

Still, Marian was always a good people person and so we have managed to work out a great routine. We even love each other now!

We play 'Catch and Fetch'. We eat together and take rides together. Although I'm sure I know how to drive, Marian won't let me and makes me stay in the back which I do, most of the time.

Maybe someday she will give me a chance to show off my driving skills.

Now, the rest of the Story:

The Hospital and Dr. O'Keefe

This letter is about when I got sick, the friends that I met, and how this book came to be.

One day, a really good day, I played "Catch and Fetch", had a great dinner, a nice nap on Marian's lap, and then slept most of the night. Marian got up early, thank goodness, and found me dead asleep on the floor. When I wouldn't get up she picked me up and rushed me right off to the doctor.

And so it was that I met Dr. Deborah A. O'Keefe at the veterinary hospital. I spent several days in intensive care while nice white-coated People Persons watched over me, petted me, and helped me not worry so much. Marian was really worried too. I heard her using the speaker phone one night as she told the doctor, "Please do all you can, this dog is all I have."

This is when I knew I was needed at home so I had to hurry up and get well so I could take care of Marian.

So, I had IVs and pills and all kinds of other stuff along with lots of watching over and, in the end, I finally got to go home. I slept for a week.

Being sick is hard work you know, not only for the sick one, but for all the People Persons around them. It's hard....hard work. In fact, I thought that I was broken, but it turns out that I was only bent.

Still, I was very sick and I was very scared and I thought that maybe I was going to die.
Fortunately, Dr. O'Keefe was very kind, caring, and very smart. She saved me and that is how I got to be home. So that is why my first book ever is dedicated to Dr. Deborah A. O'Keefe.

You see, as soon as I got better, I knew that the proper thing to do was to write a thank you note to the doctor. So I did and here it is, my very first letter:

A Letter to Dr. O'Keefe

Dear Dr. O'Keefe:

This is just a note to tell you that I am once again home. I am safe and sound in my very own house, with my very own backyard and my very own doggie door.

I am home thanks to you, your medical skills, and your kindness in saving me when I was very sick and very scared at the thought that I might die.

My people person was very scared too. She always felt better when she to talked to you on the telephone, even in the middle of the night when she couldn't sleep. I think she just needed to be assured that I was doing okay.

So I want you to know that I will be a good patient and take my pills, my naps, and I will eat my pedigree.

I am so very grateful to you for saving me. I will never forget you.

I love you!
Egypt

I thought it would be fun to take this letter on our next visit so I dressed up with a scarf and a blue balloon and off I went to see Dr. O'Keefe.

I think Dr. O'Keefe was very surprised and pleased to get the letter because she shook her head and smiled a lot. She told me and Marian that she had never ever received a letter from a dog before.

Well, that got me thinking, and so that is when I decided to keep on writing and that is how this all got started!

Please keep reading. I have so much more to tell you.

My Monroe House

After I lived in Monroe for while, I began to understand just how lucky I am. You see, I have landed in English Cocker Spaniel Retirement Heaven! ECSRH for short!

I have listened very carefully as visitors exclaim how cute and smart I am. Then they talk about all my predecessors, of which there were five! Apparently this is retirement heaven going back to the 70s.

The first was Trixie, the 'Trick or Treat" tri-colored spaniel, who had been acclaimed by the American Kennel Club as the mother of the year. She came from Marian's friend Jane Dant.
Next was Lujon Gayward Soulscott, also from Jane Dant as he was Trixie's nephew. He was AKC and had ribbons from the ring. After that was Jeremy, the rascal, who had also received ribbons.

Jeremy came from Dr. and Mrs. Ferguson from Duke University. Then came sweet Lucy from Joanne Davis in Eastland. I don't know about her ribbons but everybody said she was so sweet.

I never found any of these ribbons but, if they had as good a life as I do, they were lucky dogs. Although I can't help but think about all of these great dogs being AKC registered, I'll have to write a letter about that later.

It is too bad that these retired residents never left any notes or letters that I can find.

That's another reason why I am writing, as there is so much to say about the life of an English Cocker Spaniel. I have a mission to say the "unsaid" and maybe even say the "un-sayable."

Letter to the American Kennel Club

I've decided to share some thoughts about the American Kennel Club:

To: The American Kennel Club
From: Egypt
Subject: About this pedigree stuff

I am only five and not very polished and am feeling upset. All those pedigree dogs were supposed to be blue ribbon cockers but I haven't been able to find the ribbons. I don't have any ribbons although Marian says to me every day, "Here is your pedigree".

I say "Thank you" but then she feeds me and doesn't give me a ribbon.

I really don't understand. Why can't I join the club?

I have a couple more issues and am thinking of starting a petition with the following points:

First of all, let's talk about TAILS.

When I first met my Marian, she said, "She has a tail!" My goodness, don't all dogs have tails? How else to express joy, sorrow, excitement and uncertainly or fear? There are times when puppy eyes can't get the message out. I do understand that, since I am an English Cocker, according to the rules, I am not supposed to have a tail.

Well, who made those rules anyway, and why? I clearly remember when Dr. O'Keefe said, "She is doing so well, and oh, that tail, I think all cockers should keep their tails." So, American Kennel Club, what do you say now?

I think having a tail is a very significant method of communication in stressful times.

Like when your people person is going away. You can always tell when that is going to happen.

Just watch, your people person combs their hair, checks the coffee pot, locks all the doors, and then looks for their keys, purse, and cell phone. Then you hear, "Stay, stay, good girl."

That's when you need your tail because as soon as you hear the word 'stay', the tail should go down and you should drop to your knees and use your puppy eyes. That won't stop your people person from going out but might make them feel guilty enough to come home early.

Letting your ears flop down when your tail goes down is also a great help in making your people person feel guilty.

I feel sorry for short-eared dogs because they can't make their ears fall down, and, if they don't have a tail, they can't do the guilt trip at all.

Whoever said life was fair!

I was going to talk about 'being mixed' but, since I don't feel very mixed, I have decided not to talk about that.

Charlevoix in the Summer

When June comes it is time for my real fun time! My house up north is a mansard (like a chalet) and it sits on the beach of Lake Michigan where there is nothing but sand, water, and sunsets. How I love that place of tranquility and peace.

There is a huge deck where I play ball and there is no fence so I can wander around willy-nilly. When I jump in the lake and come back dripping all over the house. A surprised Marian will say: "You are all wet".

I say, "I know."

Then she says, "I wish you wouldn't do that".

And I say, "I am five years old and I like to jump in the lake."

Then she says, "You smell." And I say, "I know."

Then she laughs and gets a towel.

Sometimes I get a cookie, but more often than that, I just get a hug.

Everybody needs a hug especially if they have been bad!

Letter to Dr O'Keefe

When I was in Charlevoix, I thought of Dr. O'Keefe
and so I (we) went shopping and I wrote another note.

To: Marian:
From: Egypt
Subject: Take a letter

August 6, 2008
Dear Dr. O'Keefe,
I am feeling really fine and I have some records from
my special vet in Charlevoix. Her name is Lorie
DeGrazia. She knows you and said you are a great
doctor. I thought you would like to hear that.

I brought you a few things from my favorite market in
Charlevoix and I hope you enjoy them. I wanted to
bring you chocolate fudge from Kilwin's but I think
Marian ate it all. She denies this and says that she
forgot to buy it. I don't know which excuse is dumber
so I will get the fudge next time, keep it with ME, and

bring it to you on the next trip. Please let me know if this is alright. Thanks for making me well and I hope to see you soon.

Love,

Egypt

Dr. O'Keefe's Reply

Dear Egypt and Marian,

Thank you so much for thinking of me and for the yummy goodies from Charlevoix. As for the chocolate fudge; I never eat chocolate as it is toxic, you know. But I do love peanut butter fudge as it is all protein.

Fondly,

Debi O'Keefe

Summer is over, back to Monroe...

Doggie Day Care

When I got back to Monroe I went to Play and Stay for a visit. This is where Cheryl lives and where I love to go and "Stay and Play." At her Doggie Spa I get myself brushed, washed, and even an occasional pedicure.

Cheryl was very glad to see me. But then she said, "Oh, my goodness, look at you, you have sand in your ears."

I said, "umhum."

She said, "You have sand in your toes."

I said, "Umhum."

She asked, "What have you been doing?"
I said, "Body surfing in the lake."

She said, "Well, try to be more careful as you are all gummy."

I said, "Umhum, maybe next year." People persons always say obvious things.

After the visit Cheryl wrote me a note...

Dear Egypt:

I was sure glad to see you back home in Monroe. I will expect to see you regularly so you don't get all gummy again.

I still remember your very first visit to Play and Stay. You passed your Affinity Skills tests and we took you to the play room. It wasn't long after that we couldn't find you. We almost panicked as to what we would tell your people person.

Then we found you sitting proudly on the bleachers with all the stone cast dog statues. What a relief.

Fondly,
Cheryl and all the staff.

These people persons are really catching on to this letter thing.

Naturally I had to reply…

Cheryl,

Thanks for the remembrances; I remember a few things myself.

I remember our first meeting very well. The very first thing that you did was to tell Marian, "Well, that leash has got to go."

THEN you took away my twenty foot leash. I loved that leash, if you can love any leash, that is.

I used to roam around anywhere and everywhere, whenever I felt like it.

THEN you gave Marian a six-foot leash and worst of all you gave her a choker chain and put it around my neck.

THEN you showed Marian how to tug it just right, so that I had to do what I was told.

THEN you suggested I go to obedience school, and the next thing I knew I am in night school and I am only five years old!

So off I went to school and I learned the English language:

Come
Sit
Stay
Down

And the hardest word of all... **No!**

I learned that "No" means stop it right now and I learned the hard way. I was in the car, jumping back and forth from the back seat to the front seat, Marian said, "No" and I didn't stop

As a result Marian tied me down in the back seat with my leash. I am still being tied down in the back of the car. Marian told me that it was a dog rule. I don't know whether to believe her or not. What do you think?

Well, back to my learning the English language. There was also, "upstairs", "downstairs", "in the house", and "off to bed."

I was beginning to think that I had learned everything a five-year-old Cocker Spaniel needed to know when I discovered I next had to learn the American Kennel Club walk.

On the left, next to the knee, start out with the left paw and slowly match your stride to Marian's.

Walk only as fast or slow as your walker. Sit when she stops. Start when she starts: Tail up, head up, and strut. "Oh, I am so ready for the ring."

I wonder if some day the AKC will have a new division for Labradoodles, Cockapooes and the like. Then I could really join up!

Well, enough of that silly talk. I kept trying to forget all the above and just be my five year old self and that worked for a long time.

Marian is such a softie; she didn't make me do much. So, that is the way it was. You see, I had all this training and more and I mostly enjoyed it when I was doing it.

Like so many other special training events, I filed all this information away and continued on my merry way.

Life was very quiet and uneventful, filled with playful days, riding around in the car and just resting a lot. Marian gave up walking me and we mostly just played, slept and ate. I keep practicing my five year old self and I was the winning team, you better believe!

And then, to borrow a political statement from our recent candidate: "Change was coming!" Yes, I do concern myself with politics. I believe it's important to be a dog in the know. Anyway, that's when things began to happen.

Cousin Ruth and Friends

You see, Marian has a cousin who is Sister Ruth. She is an IHM sister. This stands for Sister, Servants of the Immaculate Heart of Mary. Since she is Marian's first cousin, that makes me a second cousin, once removed, I think.

Anyway, IHM's used to be called the Blue nuns because they all used to dress in blue. Now they dress in any color. In any event, I never see them as "blue" but always in shades of light green, lavender and pink as these are colors of joy and happiness, a sure sign of inner peace.

Ruth visited me regularly and I did very much enjoy seeing her. One day she brought me an angel medal and put it around my neck to keep me safe. Of course, the proper thing to do was write a thank you note, so I did:

Dear Cousin Ruth:

I do so love my angel medal that I will wear it every day and think about you.

Some day you must tell me what angel dogs do; meanwhile I will just try to be a good dog as I think that's what an angel would like me to do.

Love from Egypt

One day she brought her friend Mary Ann with her. I greeted them joyously as I greeted all visitors.

Here is the scene:

Doorbell rings, I run around and around and around to make sure Marian knows we have visitors. I bark,

bark and bark. This is my job. Marian speaks to me, not very softly:

"That is enough. Enough!".

Bark... Bark... BARK!
Marian opens the door.

My job now is to make the visitors very welcome so I launch myself up in the air and jump on them. That's so they will know how happy we are for visitors. Marian spends time untangling me and apologizing, but I don't know what for.

This is great fun!

I will mention that it appears these moments provided some shock value for Marian and she employed different trainers to help her deal with me.

The first was a nice young lady who had a pretty red harness called an Easy Walker.

You could walk me in it or tug on it to make me sit down. So the trainer put this on me and away we went down the street and back. I wondered, "Who could do anything but walk with this on?" But she took my picture, gave instructions to Marian, and said that I was cured and would walk okay now.

She told Marian to keep this on me and that I would learn to sit down.

As soon as she left, I had a puppy fit. I rolled around on the floor, pawed my face frantically, whimpered, and took it off. Later, thankfully, Marian lost it.

The next trainer was a big kind lady who worked with me every week throughout the winter.

We worked in the basement to save my feet. I walked and I sat and I stayed. She thought I was wonderful, and I was. Until she left and then I was me again.

Another trainer suggested that Marian bring a ball to the front door when the bell rang and then throw it far away until the visitors got in the house. I was too fast for that trick and it was soon given up.

As you can see, this was just going on and on and I was getting away with anything and everything I wanted to do when I wanted to do it.

Well, it was then that Cousin Ruth, who is much older and wiser than Marian, you know, brought Sister Nora and Sister Patrice over for a visit. Sister Patrice had just retired to the Motherhouse after many years of service in Florida and other places.

She had credentials from training a service dog named Davey. (His real name was Harley Davidson.) He was a golden retriever. After two years of training, Davey went off to live with his patient for whom he had been trained.

I later learned that Davey had his own power point presentation, which I thought was very impressive.

Anyway, Sister Patrice missed Davey a lot and when she met me, she thought I had real possibilities. Although I am a little too active and too old to be a service dog, Sister Patrice thought I could be a therapy dog.

Sister Patrice told me that a Therapy Dog was a lucky dog that visits around, looks pretty, and makes people smile. She said that if I was a therapy dog, I could walk around and wag my tail all the time, as long as I didn't hit anybody with it.

She also said if I was a therapy dog I could visit the nuns who love company. I love visiting so I thought I would see what I would have to do to be a Therapy dog.

Part II

My Aha Moment: Me, A Therapy Dog?

I got a special suit. Patrice made me a special collar, so when I got dressed up, it was training time. (Patrice and I are friends now, and I don't use her title anymore

Patrice contacted Therapy Dogs, Inc. to find out how I could join.

She got a lot of information in a nice little book. Of course, she had to read it to me as I still haven't learned how to read yet. Someday soon maybe, I hope.

Anyway the book said the therapy dogs share smiles and joy. I am very good at that so it will not be hard to do. That is what every good dog does.

Then I found out that in order to be registered I would have to be evaluated by a registered therapy dog evaluator. That sounded like a test, but I was not scared. I knew that sister would help me learn everything I needed to know and do.

Once that is done, I will get a red therapy dog suit and a nice medal to wear every day. There will be registered papers as well.

So next you will read all about the lessons I learned.

Lessons to learn… Behaving at home

First I had to learn to behave at home, especially when the door bell rang. I already told you what I was doing. It seems as if my welcome dance and happy barking was not truly understood by certain People Persons.

I had to remember what I learned in night school - there was a time to sit and stay on command.

It also seems it is not a good thing to bark, bark, bark. I thought I was saying Hello, Hello and Welcome. It was very hard but I learned that one bark was okay. That would let Marian know that someone was here. But that was to be the only bark.

I also learned that it is not a good thing to race out the door, down to the sidewalk and jump on the visitors. Sometimes learning is hard, but I did learn.

It was really something to learn that I couldn't sit down and bark at the same time. I wonder if all dogs know that.

Visitor Training:

After I learned what to do and what not to do, there was visitor training. Visitors are advised not to make eye contact with me or to speak to me.

They should put their hands out like so: [I really can't show you because I only have paws, but you get the message I'm sure.]

In short, they are supposed to ignore me until I settle down. They are also not supposed to pet me until I lie down or sit down and I am not supposed to jump on them.

It's all very civilized you see.

Marian gives out the lessons by email and telephone as this is very important to my future as a Therapy dog.

When the visitors act calmly, I am calm. That is good I know. Now when all the visitors are trained, I can begin to train Marian, but that will be very hard.

So, I am practicing all I know. I am walking the walk, sitting, standing on point, and always being sweet. All of these actions bring hugs and treats.

What fun it is to recognized for doing good things. Maybe I will get to do more of these things when I am not so rambunctious. I heard Marian say that.

It is going to be wonderful to be a Therapy Dog. I can hardly wait to be full time as I am so excited to be going to the Motherhouse.

I understand that a power point presentation in my honor is being fixed up for the Sisters. It will be on TV at the Motherhouse.

I wonder what Davey would think about that?

Actually, I don't think I am so special, but the work I am being trained to do most certainly is.

So even though I seem to complain a lot, I will really like it, I know.

It will be so nice to visit the Sisters. Having Ruth and Mary Ann visit me at my house is always fun. So, if I was a Therapy Dog, I could visit at their house.

I soon found out there was much more to learn.

Leash Walking:

So with my collar on and my special leash I began to practice "the walk". I was to put my head and tail up and stroll. It means I match my steps to Patrice's steps (I remembered all that from night school).

We practiced up and down the street from my house. I learned to sit on command when other walkers approached. Children run, really fast, to see me, so I sit down right away and pat my tail. Then they know I am so happy to see them.

It seems that all the People Persons like to play with my long ears and tickle me under my chin.

It took me a lot of practice, but I got it now and I am a good leash walker most of the time.

You know, in Charlevoix, on vacation I like to run around willy-nilly on the beach and just have fun, fun, fun. But now I know there are advantages to putting yourself on the leash and following the rules.

This is what most People Persons do. There is a certain satisfaction to being in tune with the real world.

This taught me that you can't live life off the leash all the time. There are benefits to walking in step with companions as you go through life.

Me: The Better Lap Dog

The next lesson was: How to be a better lap dog.

Let me tell you what kind of lap dog I am at home. I just spring up on my knees, jump and land on a lap, mostly Marian's lap. She usually says "ufff" and laughs.

I am 31 pounds you know and that's a lot of "ufff".
Well, I learned there is a gentler way that Therapy
Dogs get on laps.

Patrice showed me what to do: She would sit in the
red chair and pat the cushion next to her left knee.
Then she says "Snuggle". I learned to put my muzzle
down and stay quiet. Then when she says "Up" I put
my paws on her lap and stay still again.

If she says "okay" I put me on her lap and get petted.

So I/We practiced a lot and when I got really good at
all this, I got to go to the Motherhouse and meet the
sisters for the first time.

Visiting the Sisters

Patrice posted notices to tell everybody that a Therapy
Dog was coming to visit. She also announced that I
would only be visiting if I was invited because some of
the Sisters were afraid of dogs.

I never heard of such a thing, but I guess it is true.
In fact, it really is true. I just remembered seeing
some bad dog behavior. I saw dogs that barked at
People Persons and some even nipped.

Now, that is scary. So I will just be very gentle and
sweet and maybe the sisters won't be afraid of me.
So I got a ride and went to the Motherhouse. It was
the biggest house I ever saw and I was impressed.
We, Patrice and I went in and registered. I was in my
red Therapy Dog suit with my name on it. Everybody
smiled at me. And I was happy.

We got in a big cage. At first I was scared and I
shivered. Then I found out it was fun to go up and
down without walking. I don't shiver any more. Later,
Patrice told me it was an elevator.

Then I began my visits. We walked around and
everybody noticed me and smiled at me. I smiled
back. It seemed as if everybody liked me.

At first I only met a few Sisters. Now I am visiting forty one Sisters and am always open for new appointments.

Sister Patrice hands out the treat. She doles them out to the Sisters and they give them to me (they are counted out because I have to watch my waistline as everybody does).

All of the Sisters are special. All of the visits are special in their own way. Every room is different and every People Person Sister is different. That is inspiring.

The sisters tell me stories and I listen carefully. One Sister always gives me an ice cube. That is refreshing. Another Sister has a toy on her window seat. I go right in and get it and we play together.

Another nice place to visit is that room where Sister has a water dish and a treat for me. Yummy.

Just being there and sharing time together is the best part. Time is so precious, we need to count it and use it well always. I love being with the Sisters.

And I do love the staff. It is real fun to see them walking the halls. As soon as I see them, I flop down on my back and wiggle all around. They bend down and pet me just right.

After the visits I get to romp around in the Sisters enclosed courtyard and that is really cool. I know some of the Sisters are watching me out their windows so I always show off a little. I sort of pretend that I am on the greyhound track, so I run and race around and around and up and down.

I forget to tell you that sometimes I get to participate in physical therapy. The Sisters play with a ball, and toss it back and forth. They toss it in a basket sometimes. They were delighted to see I could do that too!

I also play soccer and indoor baseball. I belong in the Sporting Group you know. I do so love to play at anything.

I still have not been invited to the kitchen yet, and I don't understand why. Of course there must be some strange reason that I don't know about. I eat breakfast in the kitchen, at home you know. So I would be comfortable in the Sister's kitchen. Someday I must tell the Sister's that it is okay for me to eat in the kitchen.

Special Clothes on Special Days

Halloween was a very special day for me. We, Patrice and I, dressed up in identical suits. We were twins.

We sat on a bench right outside the dining room so nobody could miss us. I was number 177213 and Patrice was number 177214.

We were a begging sensation. I don't know why
Patrice wouldn't have her picture taken with me.

If I look grumpy, it is because I was. I didn't
understand why Patrice wouldn't pose with me.
Well, anyway, we did have fun. Everybody smiled as
soon as they saw us. I smiled back. I greeted all my
friends and wagged my tail a lot.

Many pictures of me were taken and you may see them on my Facebook page one day.

Patrice is very creative and has made hats and headbands for me. I have clothes for every occasion, antlers for Christmas, rabbit ears for Easter and special effects for St. Patrick's Day.

I do love football and spend all my Saturdays on the tube when the colleges play. I have a green rain suit from Michigan State and a gold suit from Notre Dame. I have sweats from U of M. Fans call it underwear and are pleading for a nicer U of M suit. Time and a new coach will tell. Isn't it interesting that my best suit is a red silk suit from Ohio State? Need I say more?

Patrice says I have more clothes than she has, but what can I say......it is what it is.

Whew, all this serious talk takes so much energy; I think we should get back to some more fun stuff and I mean English Cocker Spaniel fun stuff.

Did I ever tell you about my first blue ball?

Part III – English Cocker Spaniel Fun Stuff

My Blue Ball

This very special ball was given to me, and only me, by my friend Delphine. It is just the right size to fit in my tiny mouth, and fits in just the right way so it is partly hidden from view but just enough shows to tease the looker if they are looking for a great ball.

I have never let anybody else play with my blue ball. It goes everywhere with me and is my baby which comforts me when I am lonely, tired or sad. I think that everyone should have a friend who cares enough to give them a blue ball.

Marian, Ken, and I were sitting around playing catch and fetch when one of us, not me, suggested it would be fun to try to teach me to return the ball to the nearest waste basket. Well, I did learn and more than they had hoped for.

The blue ball can now be found in what they call "in, in, and in!"

- in the printer
- in the dishwasher
- in the bathtub
- in the closet
- in the dresser drawer
- in the paint tub
- In the suitcase.
- In the shoe

After hiding the ball I like to sit outside the latest hiding place with puppy eyes and a wagging tail hoping for attention.

Marian tries to impress me and says, "Fun is fun, but enough is enough!" Sometimes I stop but sometimes I don't.

Did I ever tell you what happened to my blue ball when I went to Charlevoix?

June 10, 2009

Dear Patrice,

As you know, I am in Charlevoix, playing catch and fetch with Marian and whomever else I can find. I am having fun, fun, fun!

My blue ball isn't here. Marian wouldn't let me bring it with me as she was afraid SHE would lose it and I would be sad if that happened and she is SO right!

Now, you may watch over my blue ball and you can play catch and fetch if you like. I know you will be careful.

Thank you for the training tips. I have done my best to train Marian, but it is still hard work.

See you soon,
Egypt

Then I got an email from Ken and this is what he said:

Hi Egypt,

Thank you for leaving your blue ball for me to play with. I am playing "In, in, in" so when you come home, you can look for it 'in'?

I know you can find it, because you find everything you ever looked for.

See ya, Ken

And now, the rest of the story...

You see, although I left my blue ball for Patrice to play with if she wanted to, Ken got it.

I got home and looked in, in, and in but I never found it anywhere.

He finally came over and come to find out, he put it 'in' under my bed. That was not part of my training!

Egad, what a bother!

You know, Ken and Marian had so much success in teaching me how to put the ball in, in, and in that they talked about teaching me to play 'Hide and Seek'. I could learn how to hide and seek but I think I am a better SEEKER than a hider.

It is true that sometimes one needs to hide, to hide from pain, from disappointments, from loss, and hide to regroup, and to think. But, it is always better to seek than to hide because the answers only come from seeking. Yes, I too am learning great wisdom.

A Letter to the Cat Next Door

Dear Kitty Poo,

I have learned a lot from you and want to thank you even though you did not know that you were teaching me good stuff.

I saw your golden paws and fluffy tail when you were sashaying and dancing around in the yard and I knew what you were doing. You shadow dance with the visitors in your yard. You pretend to see them then you pretend not to see them, and, in fact, you act like you don't even care that they are there and then whammo, you act. You spring and play catch and fetch and solve the problem.

So, I thank you, because that is how I learned. You see, most dogs just fetch. But I catch and fetch and that is special, or so they say. This is always with my blue ball, you know. Marian throws it and I usually catch it on the very first bounce.

That is the way life should be. On those rare occasions when I miss on the first bounce, I review my actions and sashay around just as you do. Sometimes I pretend to miss it, even though I actually do miss it, and sometimes I run around pretending to frantically look for my ball.

This seems to keep my people person quite engaged in our game. So, I thank you and hope you keep up the modeling behavior.
Fondly, Egypt

A Reply From the Cat Next Door

Thanks for the heads up. I'm glad I inspired you to improve your life skills. We, in cat life, have been practicing for a long time. I think a longer time than you cocker spaniels, but let's not argue about that today. It's too beautiful out there with a soft breeze, sun and lots of squirrels to tantalize.

I did want to share one shocking piece of news however. I find that you are touting your English Cocker Retirement Home and lists of AKC retirees, but did you know that your people person used to have a cat!

Yes, his name was Joseph Patrick Kitten and he lived to be seventeen years old. One story I remember clearly. JPK was called Kitty Joe and one summer he disappeared for a long time and I wondered what happened.

Well, let me tell you. His people person, (Marian) took him just to have his nails clipped but he must have ended up at the Kitty Shampoo Saloon.

Because it was so warm it was decided to clip him so he would be cool. Well, it was a horror to this long-haired gray Persian, as he ended up shaved. So, although he was very cool, he was ashamed and he stayed in the basement all of August.

Dear, dear, I thought he would never get over it but he did finally and everything turned out okay. His people person never did that again. Marian told all the other people persons with cats what happened and they all gave up shaving their cats.

My reply to Kitty Poo:
Yes, I suspected that Marian had a cat. There are no family secrets here!

When I was in Charlevoix, I counted up all the cat statues and I found five of them! One was a clay statue from Florida; one is gray that came from the Little Sisters, one with purple butterflies which would be my favorite if I could have a favorite cat, one in wood, and one in carved wood hanging on the wall.

There was, however, not one single dog statue! Maybe it's because we don't sit long enough to have one made. You cats do that pretty well. But there are no cats now, so it is all in the past. In any event, I

hear that she gave up cats when she got Lujon
Gayward Soulscott whom she called Scotty. I love
that name Lujon. It sounds like knighthood

"Thanks for telling me, Kitty Poo, but I already had
my suspicions".

A Letter From Kitty Joe

Dear Egypt,
You have been busy talking about cats. Well, this is
Kitty Joe and I will tell you the rest of the story. You
see, there was me, Kitty Joe, Papa Joe, Mama Joe
and Cookie Joe and we all lived nicely together for a
very long time.

I read that you were talking about hiding and
seeking. I can tell you about that. I learned that
game to make Marian laugh. She would peek around
the corner and then hide her head. I would run
around and find her and then disappear.

She would then peek around the corner and I would run around and find her again and we would both laugh.

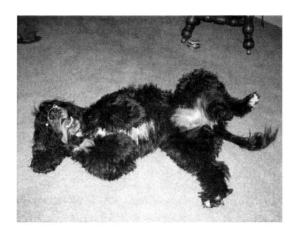

We played that game a lot. Even Mama Joe and Papa Joe would play along and we would laugh together. I hear this game is called "peek-a-boo."

Laughing is good for you. You can try it too, and laugh just like me.

A Letter for a New Puppy

I suppose you are expecting the Welcome Wagon. Well, I'm sorry to disappoint you but this letter is all that there is. If you listen well, there is good advice here which could guide you in all your future activities.

First of all, after you have accomplished the mundane things about your life, you know, going outside and doing what you need to do, never missing or messing up, you are ready for Graduate School. We are quick learners and after grade school we go right to college.

So, after puppy hood and, even during puppy hood, there are some things you should try, even if at first you don't succeed.

First of all, never lose your puppy eyes. Your inner soul peers out through them with longing and love, even if you don't feel it at the moment.

Finally, I know this sounds harsh, but you have to take care of yourself first, because if you don't take care of yourself, how can you help anyone else?

My German grandfather taught me that.

One thing to learn is position. When you want something, pant a little, give a baby whine and use the puppy eyes. Lower your ears so that you look sad.

You may also put one paw in the air and stay very still. This usually results with "Oh my, what do you want? You're so cute." Then and only then, wag your tail because you won.

Some people are very fussy about where they sleep and you should be too. It is always better to sleep in a bed, better yet, the people bed. Sometimes this is hard to work out. Try your puppy feet on the bed.

Puppies have marshmallow feet so maybe you won't be noticed. Even if you are initially rejected, wait for a moment and try again. Finally, when your people person is asleep, go ahead and get on the bed anyway. Make sure to be quiet, stay on the edges and don't sneeze.

For heaven's sake, don't try to snuggle at first as this will come later, after you receive acceptance and true love. Remember, in order to achieve goals, start small and never give up!

Here are some more thoughts for you to think about, especially goal setting:

I think you should know about growing up. It is important to learn how to bunt, that is to say, when you want something, you can't always hit a home run.

Baseball can be a little bit like the game of life. We only get nine innings, and we usually don't get extras, so you have to make the best use of them.

What does this have to do with goal setting? Well, it has to do with how you live your life. Let me explain how I see this.

I often want what I want when I want it, and I want it all. When I act like that Marian goes into her social work mindset. She tells me that I am acting like I have the "terrible two's."

I am not sure what that means but I do know that means I have to 'chill out' and try to get what I want in a different, maybe a little more subdued way. I like to win and so do most people. So, a soft approach is often far superior to "I want what I want when I want it."

There is an American Mantra that tells us to live, live and live in the present moment. But you also need to pick the right moment.

That is what grown ups do. Sometimes you can get a home run and sometimes you can't. In order to win, sometimes you have to learn an alternate strategy, like bunting. You see when you or your coach decides you should bunt, this is an indicator that in order to win you must take smaller steps. You decide the costs and consequence of bunting vs. the home run swing. So if you can win by bunting, why not take a different swing at life?

I am trying this out and will let you know how it works. You can also try it. It is like slowing down and choosing the moment.

One Final Thought for a New Puppy

Don't do as I do, just do what I say. This is some good advice about Cocker Spaniel sins and I have tried them all! So trust me, I know what I am writing about!

Don't drool, whatever you do, as your people person hates this.

Don't bark too much - it is not your life's work to patrol the street.

Don't be caught on the counter trying out the pasta dish.

For heaven's sake, don't be found on the kitchen table trying out the meatloaf.

Now let me tell you why: I did all of these and many more. My people person found me and I had the poor judgment to growl and she said, "You do that one more time and I will give you something to growl about."

How does a growl become a howl? I don't think I want to find out.

So, as I said, don't do as I do, just do as I say. Good luck, little puppy!

Part IV – Conclusions and Epilogue

I need to tell everyone that all my paper work has been approved. I have passed all my tests and I am a fully certified therapy dog!

I am the first Therapy dog at the IHM Motherhouse in Monroe, Michigan. I have my license tag from the city, my Therapy Dog tag, and my angel medal.

I jingle and jangle, like a real canine. Oh my goodness, I am so happy, I don't know what to do.

I also have other credentials. I have an award for being the best Dog in the fire drill at the IHM Motherhouse. Now, the fact that I was the only dog in the fire drill does not diminish the significance of the award. (Marian said that.)

Honors for best dog during fire drill

to

My second award was from the Project Second Chance. This is a program that places stray dogs and puppies with young people who socialize, train and love these lost dogs. Then they become adoptable and they find their "People Person".

You know, everybody should have a People Person to take care of.

Project Second Chance sponsors special events with games and contests for both pets and People Persons.

At one of these events I entered a contest for "Waggiest Tail"

Five of us were in the ring and I won. One of the onlookers admiring us said, "She never stops, does she?" And I never will.

In fact in 2010 I entered and won first prize for "Waggiest Tail" again. Sad to say there were two other events that I didn't win.

First there was "Best Treat Catcher" and I only came in second. If only Marian had let me practice 24-7 like I wanted to it might have been a different story.

The really sad thing was the second event: Best Kisser and I didn't even need to practice for that. But I came in second again and that is so sad I can't even talk about it.

I hate to end on a sad not, but there is always next time in life to do better. You just have to pick yourself up and try again. You know I will.

Now that works for contests. But if you are talking about serious life events, first you have to decide: "What do I need? And what do I want?

If the answers don't match you better rethink, because you are on the wrong track. That's when you have to go back and see where you fell off the track.

And staying on the right track is all that matters in life. I keep that at the top of my mind and set up my goals accordingly. You can do this too. It leads to a better life.

I have told you most of my thoughts and stories now. So after two years I am ready to close this book.

I want to thank everyone who wrote to me and helped me. I hope you enjoyed hearing from me. In closing, Marian and I again want to recognize the goodness of Dr. Debi O'Keefe who inspired me to begin writing.

And we want to acknowledge the personal energy, professional dedication of all the veterinarians, technicians, as well as the support staff of veterinary clinics everywhere.

The love and care they so graciously give to our extended family members is truly an inspiration.

Marian and I truly enjoyed writing this and wonder if all the family pets could talk and or write, what all would be said. If your dog wrote, what would be his or her story? And what if cats could write?

You know, we started out to create a power point presentation for the IHM sisters and one thing led to another. We still want to create the presentation and we will. We feel really inspired and have great ideas of what might be done in the future:

We thought about beginning a Dogapedia or better yet an Egyptapedia.

We thought about searching the internet to see who else is writing "Letters from the Dog"

We even thought about searching the internet to see who might be writing "Letters from the Cat". But who wants to take on the feline population of the world?

We even thought about posting on Twitter but dogs don't twitter for heavens sake.

If anything you have read here has helped you look or think about your dog in a different way, please share those special moments.

You can find "Letters From the dog" on Facbook and you can share your thoughts there. We would love to hear from you and you can be a forever friend.

Even kitties can write us here and we would enjoy their stories too.

Egypt and Marian
Letters From the Dog

Epilogue:

Well, I suppose you may have wondered what my People Person thinks about all these stories of mine. I guess I should explain that I am very blessed to have a wonderful People Person who has the time to indulge my fantastic lifestyle and me. Sometimes I wonder what she is really thinking. And now I have the chance to find out...

Some thoughts and letters
from my People Person

Well, yes, I finally get a moment to share, and I do have some memories to relate.

First, I will tell you that I am referred to as Egypt's owner but I often wonder who owns whom!

And you need to know that this English Cocker Spaniel, who was too fat, too wild and who has a tail (heaven forbid!) is the light of my life.

She brought me a life, and you will see what fun we have together.

What follows are stories on life with this exceptional dog, my Egypt, the Author of "Letters from the Dog."

Squeaky Addiction – Well, She has it!

Somebody, I won't say who, brought over a red ball squeaky toy. This person left it on Egypt's dresser - which used to be mine but is now the toy chest.

Did I ever mention that she has the dog world's best nose for rubber? Yes, she does, as she can sniff out a toy wherever it is. If it is in your pocket, she smells it. If it is in a grocery bag, she smells it. If a friend comes over and brings a gift she smells it and in all cases, she wants it right now!

This is what happened this morning...

We shared our breakfast. Well, not really, as she doesn't share her plate but expects me to share my plate, which of course I do. Then we have a little nap, me with my head back in my red chair, her asleep on my lap.

When she is ready, we get up. She adopts her stance, looks really serious and points her head towards the kitchen and takes a few tentative steps. She is always looking back at me. So, I say, "What is it?" She continues to take steps, so I follow.

Now she leads me to the master bedroom. I find, in a circle on the rug, the blue ball, the white toy and she stands in that circle and points to the dresser. You see, yesterday I made a terrible mistake. I opened up the dresser drawer and not only found the red squeaky toy but actually picked it up and gave it to her!

I am still suffering sqeekieitis from yesterday and today she wants it again!

What is a mother to do?

Trying My Patience

She has been asking to go downstairs, with the stance and the eyes and the pointing of the nose, the doggie two step and other doggie gestures.

So, even though I am not dressed and am in robe and slippers, I say, "Okay, downstairs" and away she goes with me, the follower.

So we get to the top of the stairway, I turn on the light, the blue ball is at my feet and I say, "Well, bring it" and I start downstairs.

I am in robe and slippers and this is a tedious task. I get downstairs and there is no Egypt. I settle into my chair and call her but there is no response.

I wait.

I call again, "Egypt!"

I do hear a small bark but still no Egypt so I traipse upstairs to find there is no Egypt anywhere.

I look all around; I go outside (even though it is twelve degrees).

I call again. I get no Egypt, no answer, nothing.

I go inside and look around again. I even look in the garage and am seriously thinking about phoning for help because Egypt is gone.

Then she appears with that look that says, "Where have you been? Where were you when I needed you?" She leads me to the master bedroom, goes in the master bathroom, and goes on point at the master closet door. I open the door and there is her white dog toy. She picks up her toy, marches out of the room, goes to the basement stairs and gives me the "lets us go downstairs" look.

"Not on your life!" I say and retreat to the red chair in the living room.

Now, do you wonder why I wonder who owns whom?

It looks like a draw! Well, that may not exactly be true.

You may have guessed that life with this "Egypt" is not always a draw. She is usually the winner and I do admit she is just a little spoiled.

All of us people persons often over indulge our dogs and cats. We are rewarded with unconditional love and loyalty that comforts and inspires us to be better humans.

Some great philosopher once said something like this, "If I can be as good a friend as my dog is, I will be a better person". We have so much to learn from the animal kingdom.

In Egypt's closing notes she invited you to write us on Facebook. I do have more thoughts and emails to share with you and we would love for you to share your experiences with us.

Thanks for reading.

Marian and Egypt.